THE CHRONICLES OF
OLLIE
and
RAVEN

Fulton Books, Inc.
Meadville, PA

Published by Fulton Books 2021

ISBN 978-1-64952-943-5 (paperback)
ISBN 978-1-64952-944-2 (digital)

Printed in the United States of America

THE CHRONICLES OF
OLLIE
and
RAVEN

BOOK 1: THE BEGINNING

D.C. Whitlock

CHAPTER 1

"Ollie! You are going to make us late!" Mom called up the stairs.

"One minute!" Ollie shouted, not wanting to leave his room.

See, Ollie and his parents were moving to Colorado from Georgia, and he was sad to leave his cool room and all his friends and his school. Well, maybe not his school!

"Ollie, I won't ask again, come on already!" Mom came up to his room to see him sitting on the floor of his room looking at pictures of his friends on his phone.

"Mom, I don't want to go. I'm going to miss my friends so much. I'm going to be so lonely!" he said hunching over with sadness."

"Oh, sweetie, you don't need to worry, you will make so many new friends in Colorado you will forget all about missing the ones here. The new school you will be going to has so many kids your age, and it's in the mountains. Ollie, can you believe it?"

"That is cool," he said, "I've never seen a mountain in real life before."

Mom smiled. "Plus there will be snow!"

Ollie jumped up excited. "Snow? I totally forgot there was snow, I've never seen snow before!"

"Plus, the neighborhood we will be living in has so many kids to play with, and our new home has a huge backyard covered in rocks and trees. It will take you months to explore."

"Really?" He smiled.

"Of course!" Mom exclaimed. "We wanted you to have the biggest backyard we could find! Once we clear out a little of the land, Dad promised to build a tree house and a swing."

"Maybe I could get a dog to explore with me?"

Mom got up and smiled. "I'm not sure, sweetie, let's ask your dad when we are in Colorado, okay? Come on, let's go get in the car we have a long drive ahead of us."

Ollie and his mom walked out of the room, and he looked back. "Bye, room, I'll miss you!" They got in the car and started driving away. *How will I ever like living in another place?* he wondered as he sat back in his seat on his way to Colorado.

CHAPTER 2

The drive was long and boring. "Are we there yet?" Ollie asked for the tenth time after an hour of driving.

"Not yet, bud, Colorado is still twenty more hours of driving. We will be there in a few days. We still have to drive through three more states to get to Colorado."

Ollie sat back and groaned, "Dad, I'm bored. There's nothing to do!"

"Nonsense, there is plenty to do!" Mom said. "We could play slug bug, or we can play the license plate game."

"Yeah!" Ollie exclaimed. "I remember playing that with Jensa and my friends Jacob, Suzie, Jeremy, and Daniel! It was so fun! We should have brought them," Ollie said, then realizing he will not be coming back to Georgia for a while.

Tearing up and sitting back in his seat, Mom grabbed his leg and squeezed gently. "Aww, honey, it's going to be okay. You will see them again, plus you guys are all going to write letters and chat online as often as you can, come on let's play!"

Ollie wiped the tears away and gave a small smile, still really missing his buddies. "Maybe later, Mom, I think I want to just listen to music right now," Ollie said quietly, pulling out his headphones and lying back, looking out the window and looking at the grey clouds that were about to come overhead. "How will I ever find friends as awesome and cool as them? I've known them my whole life." Looking down, turning on his favorite playlist, he and his friends all made together, Epic Fantasy Wilderness Music is what they named it. See, Ollie and his friends didn't play sports or played video games all day, they loved being outside using their imagination.

Fighting goblins, sword fighting each other, finding treasure, and slaying dragons with magic. Ollie was the brains of the gang writing down the different missions and adventures they could go on. Ollie gazed out the window as he remembered their last quest together.

"Look out, Jacob the Great, there are arrows raining down on us!" Ollie shouted, tackling Jacob, both covered in painted cardboard armor. A few sticks flew by their heads and landed right next to them.

"You saved my life, Ollie the Great. However, are we going to break through and save Princess Twinklesnap?" Jacob said, giggling at the name. A few more sticks went over the log they were hiding behind.

"Give it up, you pesky Knights! I, Commander Jeremy will never let Princess Twinklesnap go free!"

He shouted from the tree house he was sitting in, "Captain Scary Suzie, release more arrows and bombs this time!"

Suzie shouted, "Take this you, dorks!" as she threw more sticks and a few water balloons out over the log.

"Hey, cut it out you're getting my armor wet Suzie!" Jacob said, looking over the log.

"Dude, stay in character. You know the rules!" she said back to him, throwing another balloon.

"Fall back to the trees," Ollie said dramatically taking off as fast as he could and Jacob trailing behind him.

Both out of breath, Ollie peeked over the trees. "Okay, I think they are distracted with us. I'll call in the secret weapon." Ollie puts his hands together and starts cooing like an owl. "*Coo, coo, coo*! All right, Jacob the Great, are you ready to go back out and vanquish this evil?" Ollie said grabbing a few sticks and getting out his cardboard sword.

"Are you sure this will work?" Jacob said, watching the paint run on his wet armor sadly.

"It totally will, the Elf King is the better climber and will get up there quietly while we keep the attention of the evil doers."

"Help me, help me, I am so scared and so helpless," came an unhappy voice from the tree house.

"Daniel, come on, do better than that!" Suzie said whacking him with a stick.

"Ow, hey cut it out, okay, okay," Daniel raised his voice higher to sound like a girl, "Oh, dear me, help me, help me, it is I, Princess Twinklesnap!" All the kids started laughing hearing him. "Whoever will come save me from these evil goblins!" Daniel added dressed in a white sheet with a crown and a long wig tied to a chair.

"Never fear, Princess, for Ollie the Great and Jacob the Great are here to save you. Charge!" Ollie and Jacob started running over to the base of the tree house throwing the sticks at the walls. Suzie jumped down and drew her sword. Her and Jacob started the epic sword fight as Ollie threw sticks at the tree house.

"Got you!" Suzie shouted as she hit Jacob in the chest with her sword."

Arrrggh, no I'm dying," Jacob said, grabbing her sword and putting it between his arm like he was stabbed. "I die protecting the princess I love." Falling over as he laughed at what he said.

"How dare you kill my brother!" Ollie said, running up to Suzie, and poked her with his sword.

"Aww, come on I wasn't ready!" Suzie said angrily.

"Stay in character!" Jacob whispered at her.

"Ugh fine," she said, falling over. "Aghhh, he got me! Curse you, knight of Vardosh!"

Ollie stood at the base of the tree house and smiled as he saw Jensa climbing up from behind. "Give her up, evil commander, there's no escape!" Ollie shouted.

"You fool! If you don't let me escape, then the princess shall be hit with a bomb!" Jeremy said, holding a giant water balloon over his head right next to Daniel.

"Hey wait, what no!" Daniel said, trying to scoot away in the chair he was trapped in. "Stop, Ollie, back up!"

"See I have won! Surrender or she perishes," Jeremy said, smiling.

"You have forgotten one thing, evil commander," Ollie said, backing up. "My treaty with the elves is stronger than ever!"

Jensa jumped down from the roof of the tree house, rolled over in a somersault and poked the water balloon Jeremy held over his head soaking him completely. "Oh, cold! Or I mean, aww, what nooooooo!" Jeremy screamed in a high pitch as he jumped off the tree house and laid down, "I've been beaten."

Ollie and Jensa raised their swords. "Hurray we saved the day!"

Jensa untied the Princess. "I am here for you, Princess Twinklesnap," she said giggling.

"Okay, it's over now. The end!" Daniel said, pulling off the sheet and wig. "Why did I have to be the Princess? There are two girls here and one is playing a King? Come on, that's not fair. Ollie, you wrote this story all wrong!" He said as Jensa and Daniel jumped to the ground.

"He has a point," Jensa remarked. "Come on, Ollie the Great and Jacob the Great? Neither of you could have thought of something else?"

Ollie rolled his eyes at them. "Hey, you know the rules, we all arm wrestled, and the winner got to pick who the damsel in distress was! And we considered it, yes, but in the end, Jacob and I are just both so great."

"Yeah!" Jacob added as Ollie and him high fived.

"But Jensa is eleven, that's the only reason she was the winner!" Daniel complained.

"Hey, I beat you too!" Suzie said to Daniel, punching him on the arm. "If you do not want to be the princess, you better be stronger next time!" They all laughed. They all started walking back to Jacob and Suzie's house.

"When do you leave again Ollie?" Jeremy asked.

"We leave in two weeks Dad says," he said softly.

"Why do you have to leave, you always have the best stories for us to play. It's going to be so boring without you here!" exclaimed Jensa.

"I know, I don't want to go, it's like over a thousand miles away! It's basically the other side of the world, I bet there will be nothing to do in Colorado," Ollie said blandly.

"Yeah, we are all really sad to see you go." Jacob said.

"Don't worry guys, I wrote like ten more adventures, so you still have them after I leave. Mom wrote our new address down and said we all can start writing each other! Let's talk about something else," Ollie said. "Last one to the house has to be the princess next time!" he said, pushing Daniel down, and they all took off running and laughing.

"Hey! That's not fair!" shouted Daniel.

"Ollie, Ollie!" Mom shouted, tapping his headphones startling Ollie. "Hey, we stopped for lunch, are you awake?"

"Oh, sorry, Mom," Ollie said, taking off his headphones. "I was just lost in thought. I'm coming," he said unbuckling his seatbelt and hopping out of the car. *Colorado is going to be the worst*, he thought. Still thinking about his friends as they walked in the restaurant for lunch.

CHAPTER 3

The long drive did not help Ollie's mood being cooped up in the back seat. Occasionally, he played a few games with Mom and Dad, but everything reminded him of Georgia and his friends. It rained most of the drive through every state, making it gloomy and dark outside. The farther they got, the less Ollie liked it around him. The last state they had to drive through was Kansas, and it was nothing but plains and flatness. Ollie thought he was going to be bored out of his mind forever. He was used to everything being covered in green grass and trees everywhere, most of them so thick you can barely see through them. His old house was so cool, he lived right next door to his cousin Jensa. They had a tree house and a forest in the backyard full of ponds, caves, and streams; all there to explore and write down all the fantasy adventures the gang would have.

As they pull onto their street, Ollie was in a bad mood, he did not like Colorado already; the sky was covering the mountains in a late spring fog to bring a chill and gloominess to everything. He looked around sad because there were not enough trees for him. He was freezing already and didn't want to move at all, so in the car, he decided his life was going to be playing Battle Blocks Ultra on his phone instead of exploring dumb Colorado. As Mom and Dad started unloading the car, he went into the house, it was bigger than the last house.

"Where is my room?" he asked looking up the stairs.

"This time your room will be in the basement, bud," Dad said. "It's the same size as our room, so you will have so much more space now!"

"Whatever," Ollie said, walking downstairs as he played on his phone.

Dad shook his head. "I don't understand ten-year-old kids, all they want to do today is play on their phone, text, or watch videos!"

"Give him some time. He will warm up," Mom said as she set down boxes. "It's the first day, he just needs to get settled and he will be back to normal."

Ollie opened the door to his room; it's so dark he can barely see. He switched on the light and looked around his room. "Too dark and musty," he mumbled, walking around to his window to let the air in, hearing the kids a few houses away playing with their dog and laughing. Ollie remembered what mom said and ran upstairs into the kitchen where Mom and Dad were unpacking plates. "Can we get a dog?" He blurted out before catching his breath. "We could name him Tucker, and I'll teach him so much! How to sit, how to shake, how to roll over, and how to play dead. It will be great. We will be best friends! I promise I'll walk him and feed him and clean up after him please, please, please!" Ollie begged. Mom looked at Dad with a sad look.

"Hey, bud, come sit by me," Dad said. "So, the man we are renting the house from is a great guy, he gave us a great deal, but one of the things he didn't allow was a dog. I tried to convince him, I really did, Ollie, but he wouldn't change his mind about allowing dogs in the house. I'm sorry."

"That's not fair!" Ollie shouted. "Can we just get a dog and leave him outside?"

"Sweetie, it snows and gets super cold here in the winter," said Mom.

"In a few years, we will have our own house, and we will get a dog. I promise," Dad said, nudging Ollie hoping that cheers him up.

"This isn't fair! I didn't want to move here! I hate Colorado! I hate this place!" Ollie shouted as he ran to his room and slammed the door crying.

CHAPTER 4

Three weeks pass, they are all unpacked. Dad started at his new job, and Mom set up her office to work from home. "Okay, sweetie," Mom said to Ollie, "when I am at work, I won't be able to play with you. I'll be busy today with work and won't be able to be bothered unless it's an emergency, okay?"

"Whatever," Ollie said not looking up from his phone.

"Okay, please do more than play on that thing all day," she said to him as she shut the door to her office.

"Whatever, there's nothing else to do in this dumb house," he muttered.

After lunch, he walked outside to sit on the front porch. "Some summer this is starting off to be." He pouted as he sat and watched the cars go by. He heard those kids again down the street playing with the dog. "Maybe they will let me play too," he said excitedly getting up and running over to the sound of the kids. He ran down the street four houses down seeing a group of kids playing with the dog he has been hearing. A group of three kids that look like his age and two teens, one of them holding the dog on a leash. Ollie sees the dog, it's a golden retriever! He loves those dogs. He saw the kids looking at him, he turned beet red feeling very shy, he walked by the house a little bit. "I don't know these people, what am I thinking? I hope they invite me over." He stopped and turned around walking slower by the kids this time, casually looking at the dog trying not to seem interested.

"Hello," one of the kids his age said.

"Are you the kid that just moved in a few houses down?" the girl asked.

"Yeah, my name is Ollie, we are from Georgia," he said shyly looking at the ground.

"My name is Victoria," she said with a big smile on her face, pointing at the other two kids, "this is Jeffery, but you can call him Jeff. And this is Jonathan."

"I can introduce myself, Victoria, sheesh" Jonathan blurted out angrily. "And call me Jon not Jonathan!"

20

Victoria rolled her eyes. "He's only mad 'cause my older brother won't let him hang out with them even though he's thirteen. Come sit with me?" Ollie walked over and sat in the grass with the trio.

"See, over there is Jeff's and mine's brother, Steve and Todd. They are both sixteen. I am ten and a half, Jeff is ten how old are you?

"I'm ten and a half too," Ollie said louder, getting a little comfortable.

"Oh, great another baby on this neighborhood," Jon said, rolling his eyes.

"Shut up, Jon, why are you still here?" Jeff said.

"Because I wanted to see Steve's new dog, I bet I could train it for him if he wants, I have two dogs at home," Jon said proudly bragging. They watched as the two teens were trying to get the dog to sit and shake across the yard.

"Will they let us pet him?" Ollie asked.

"I'm not sure yet," Victoria said impatiently. "They won't let us near him, Steve just got him from the shelter, and my Mom said they need to make sure it's not mean before the younger kids get to be around him. He looks all fluffy and happy and is the cutest dog ever. I don't see any meanness!" The dog started barking loud over excited jumping up on Steve.

"See, that's aggression!" Jon said jumping up and walking over.

"Hey, Jonny, stop. I already told you to wait over there. We don't want you kids to get hurt"

"I can help if you guys want," Jon blurted out loudly, still walking over.

"Stop! Either get back with the other kids or go home!" Steve said, holding the dog on the leash. Jon stopped and slowly turned around blushing. Victoria and Ollie were both giggling he got in trouble.

"What are you laughing at, you babies?" Jon shouted mad. "Why are you even here kid? We don't need anyone else making the dog nervous. We don't know you!"

"Stop that, Jonathan," Victoria said, standing. "You are being too loud. It's going to upset the dog."

"Do not tell me what to do!" Ollie stood up too.

"Hey, be quiet. You will make the dog nervous. They can sense when someone's upset." The dog started barking and jumping up on the teens again.

"Easy, boy," Steve said.

Jon pushed Ollie into Victoria making them fall. "Don't tell me what to do! I don't like you already!" Jon shouted too loud. Making the dog jump slipping out of his collar and ran after the kids, the kids screamed as the dog came inches away from them. Steve tackled the dog just in time, all of them scared. Steve got his collar on and held him tight.

"What on earth are you guys thinking? He is scared and nervous, why are you yelling?"

Before anyone could say anything, Jon pointed at Ollie, "It's his fault he kept yelling, and he pushed Victoria down!"

"No, I didn't," Ollie turning red, embarrassed.

"Kid, I don't even know who you are, but please don't ever push my sister. Please leave!" Steve said angrily.

"Steve, no," Victoria said.

"Yeah, get out of here!" Jonathan sneered. Ollie took off running to his house tears streaming down his face. Running inside, slamming the door, taking off to his room, and falling on his bed burying his face in his pillow.

Mom came into his room. "Ollie, are you okay? I heard the door slam, what's wrong?" she said, rushing over to him. "Are you hurt? What's the matter?"

"I'm not hurt, Mom, the kids down the street yelled at me and told me to go away. All I wanted to do was play with the dog!" he said, crying into the pillow.

"Oh, sweetie, I'm so sorry. I didn't know you went down there. Here, let me go talk to their mother."

"No, Mom, please don't do that. That will only embarrass me more! I'll be okay. I just want to stay inside now."

"Okay, Ollie, I'm sorry that happened. I'm sure it was a misunderstanding, and they will let you play soon."

"Yeah, okay, Mom."

"I need to get back to work. I'll see you in a little bit, okay?" She kissed his head and walked out of his room.

Ollie sat up, opened the window, and listened as he heard the dog barking. "So much for making friends in Colorado. Whatever, I'll just be alone here forever. I don't care."

CHAPTER 5

That night, Dad walked in the door, and Ollie heard him bump something as he walked through the front door. Ollie's Mom knocked on his door, "Ollie, can you come up here, we have something for you!"

Ollie ran up the stairs and saw an animal cage behind his dad's legs. "Hey, bud, so your mom told me what happened today, I'm so sorry that happened. Teenagers can be so mean. I'm sorry, everything is so new right now, so your mother and I talked today, and we want you to have a friend this summer in Colorado, so we asked the landlord and he agreed, so I went by the shelter today and got a friend for you!" He bent down and opened the cage.

"You got me a dog?" Ollie shouted excitedly, but out walked a little black cat, trotting over to Mom's feet. A cute little thing, at most four pounds heavy, ears bigger than her head, and eyes bright

yellow and deep black constantly wide as if she is always ready for an attack.

"A cat?" Ollie said, disappointed.

"Yeah, bud, she's five months old. I got her from the shelter, they said she's super outgoing and loves kids!"

"What do you do with cats? They are so boring, they sit around sleeping and scratch you all the time and look at you with creepy eyes," he said as the little black cat just sat by Ollie's dad staring at him with her big yellow eyes. Ollie stared back at her, but he felt as if she was trying to peer into his soul or scanning him for something. "Super weird," Ollie said taking a step back. "You can't even go outside with them," he said, still not getting close to her.

Ollie's Mom looks at him. "Yes you can, she has been trained to walk on a leash." Holding up a small harness. "You can still have your adventures, just give her a try!" Mom reaches down to pet her, the meows so soft and started rubbing all over Mom's legs. "Aww, such an adorable Princess," Mom said in a baby voice. "Here, Ollie, reach your hand out she's so much softer than a dog."

Ollie bends down to pet the cat, "What's her name?"

"Well, the shelter called her Princess, but if you can think of another name that suits her better, you can change it," Dad said.

Ollie reached out his hand, "Here kitty, kitty, kitty." Princess smelled his hand, chirped, and batted his hand hissing, then ran away under the couch to hide from him as if her life depended on it. "No, Princess, it's fine," Ollie said unhappily.

"She will like you, don't worry. She just has to get to know you," Mom said.

"It's fine," he said, "I don't care if she does or not," as he walked back to his room.

29

CHAPTER 6

The next day, Ollie waved goodbye to his dad as he drove off and watched his mother walk into her office and shut the door. He saw Princess by the stairs sitting, watching him intently almost squinting at him. He walks right by her and mumbles, "Well, another boring day in Colorado, creepy little cat," as he grabs his phone to play a game. Laying on his bed, not noticing the little black cat walking into his room, she meowed to get his attention, he looked down unimpressed. "Go away, Princess, I'm busy with my game."

He rolled over on his bed, Princess jumped on the bed and sat on the corner. "So, you are just going to play with the little bright box all-day, small human?" Ollie paused his game and looked around thinking he heard his Mom say something, he heard nothing else and went back to his game. "Excuse me, small human, I asked you a question," the voice said again.

Ollie paused his game again and looked over; the cat is looking right at him, he looked back. "No, there's no way he said." He leaned over to the cat and said, "Princess?"

"Eww, stop, back away, your breath is horrible, did you just lick yourself?" said the cat backing up a little.

"Whoa!" He jumped back. "How are you talking? Cats can't talk!" Ollie shouted falling out of his bed backing away from Princess.

"Of course not, I'm not talking, tiny human, I am using my mind to speak to your mind, duh!"

"This has to be a joke, is Mom trying to prank me?" Ollie said loudly walking upstairs knocking on her office door. "Mom, jokes over!"

Ollie's mom opens the door with an angry look on her face. "Ollie, what do you need? I am in the middle of a meeting, I asked you to keep it down now, please hush!" She shut the door as Ollie turned around confused.

Walking slowly down the stairs, he peeked into his room at the cat who is lying on her back paws stretched out snickering looking at Ollie. "This can't be real," he said.

"Oh, this is all real all right," she said, sitting up and walking over to where Ollie was sitting. "I am as real as you and your big humans talk."

"How?" he asked.

"I don't want to confuse your tiny brain, but I am a being of magical greatness here on a very important mission to this planet," she spoke proudly fluffing out her fur. He slowly inched closer to her reaching out his hand to touch her. She stood up and swatted his hand away, "Hey don't touch me, that's so rude just trying to touch someone without permission, I don't know where those grubby little hands have been!" she said swatting his hand again.

"But you are a cat, you are small and not even fully grown yet."

"I take this form to fool my enemies, I am hundreds of years old, and when I am ready, I will show my true self!"

Ollie smiled at the cat. "I don't think a cat named Princess has enemies."

She walked over and got close to his face, "I could turn you into a blob of goo with this paw." Holding up a paw and touching his nose, then started licking her paw as if it were dirty. "If you ever call me Princess again, that was my prison name. I am Raven, Dark Lord of All!"

"Raven? I like that name," he said holding out his hand. "My name is Ollie." Shaking hands and paws, Raven looked amused.

"I don't usually name my pets, but I suppose Ollie is okay, small human."

"Wait, I'm not your pet, you are my pet!"

Raven strutted back to the bed. "Oh really? Then tell me why you clean up my poop and feed me whenever I want with treats multiple times a day? I own all three of you!" She laughed sitting like a little loaf on the bed.

"No, that's what you do to a pet, they can't take care of themselves, we take care of you!" he said, sitting on the bed.

"I'll let you think that for now, Ollie the small human," Raven said, amused as she laid down crossing her front paws. "Now tell me, why do you look at this tiny bright box all the time? Ever since I got here, you and the other two big humans have looked at these tiny little boxes all day." She said sniffing his phone. "Do these dispense your food when you are hungry?"

Ollie laughed, "No they are phones, we can call other people and text with them and play games whenever we want." He turned it on for her.

"Call? Text? If we are to spend time together, I will ask you to not make up words," she said, squinting at him.

"Hey, wait so can my parents hear you too?" Ollie asked, still confused.

"I can talk to whoever I desire, but I choose not to talk to them, so only you can hear me for now."

"Maybe I should take you to the neighbor kids and show them I have a talking cat! Then they will think I'm cool and let me play with their dog!"

"A dog? What is a dog?" she asked, lying down on a blanket.

"You know, a dog? Man's best friend? All different colors and sizes, they bark?" Ollie said, showing her a picture on his phone.

"Ollie," Raven said as she started to yawn, "Man's best friend is the paper in the bathroom, what you just showed me on your phone is a Doggett, they rule the land of Haltaki, they are a very stupid ruler if you ask me," she snorted.

"So, what now?" Ollie asked. "What exactly can I do with a talking cat? Mom and Dad will so not believe me!"

"Well, after my nap, I shall have you take me out to the land around this base of operations to look for the evil that usually follows me around, but you should not tell anyone you can hear me, they will not understand with their little minds, humans are so simple-minded. It's almost insulting keeping a few of you around."

"Hey now," Ollie said, "be nice or no treats." He smiled.

"Whatever," the little cat said squinting, "now leave me, I must rest for my scouting trip later."

"But this is my room." Ollie said. He heard a low growl coming from Raven.

"Get out," she said growling louder.

"Okay, okay! Grumpy, I'll come back in a little bit!"

CHAPTER 7

Ollie's mom walked in the kitchen and saw Ollie looking for something all around the house. "Did you lose something, sweetie?" she asked, getting a snack.

"Yeah, I'm looking for Raven's harness, did you set it somewhere?" he asked, shoving his head under the couch looking for it.

"You mean, Princess?

"No, Mom, she likes to be called Raven, that's her name."

Mom laughed. "Oh, she likes to be called Raven? Did she tell you that?," Mom said jokingly as she handed him the leash.

"She did!" Ollie said sitting at the table. "She told me her name is Raven, Dark Lord of All."

Mom smiled at Ollie. "Is that so? Raven? I like that name, where is Raven at now?"

"She is resting right now, but when she wakes up, she wants to scout out her backyard for evil and places to look out she said," Ollie said to his mom.

"Oh, the imagination you have, sweetie." She laughed kissing his head walking back up to her office. "Just be careful out on your scouting mission," she said, "Dad said there could be some spiders out there so be careful."

"It's not my imagination, she told me herself!'

"Okay, hun," Mom said as she closed her office door.

CHAPTER 8

A few hours later, Ollie walked into his room. "Hey, are you going to sleep all day?"

Raven snorted, opening her eyes then squinted at Ollie. "You dare disturb my sleep?" she slowly got up and stretched. "That will cost you when you least expect it," she said, slowly cleaning her paw. Ollie walked over with the harness. "Okay, let's get this put on."

"No!" she hissed and jumped up. "I do not want to wear the forbidden belt of restriction! My magic won't work when I am wearing it!" She started backing up.

"Oh, come on you are joking, you will be fine." Ollie picked her up and put the little blue harness on her. "Well, don't you look cute," he said chuckling. Raven gave him the meanest look ever, glaring at him with her deep yellow eyes.

"This won't work, how will I transform?"

"What are you talking about?" Ollie looked at her walking to the door.

"I can't explain it lets just go," she said, walking to the door. They started walking out to the backyard, starting with a big patch of grass leading into a thick group of trees as far as they could see.

"Not bad. Let us walk into the mystical forest," she said, tugging on the leash.

"I'm coming," he said, running along by her. They walked into the trees covered in leaves covering up the sun.

"It sure is dark here," Ollie asked, slowing down. "There could be wild animals in here, we should go back!"

"Oh, calm down, human," Raven said. "I will take care of you if anything happens."

"You are no dog," Ollie sighed, "A dog would protect me and keep me safe."

"Will you stop with talking about a dog? There is nothing special about a dog," Raven snapped.

Ollie stopped walking. "I would even trade a talking cat for a dog! Now let's go back inside." Pulling of the leash.

"If that's how you feel, then it's time for me to be done with you," Raven said, then suddenly, she jumped and bit Ollie on the hand making him drop the leash.

"Ow!" he screamed as she takes off running deeper into the woods. "Get back here, you stupid cat!" Ollie ran after her as fast as he could barely keeping up with her. He stepped on a log and slipped on the moss smacking his head and began rolling down the hill scratching and cutting himself.

CHAPTER 9

Ollie groaned as he sits up from the ground. He tore his pants and shirt and had so much mud and leaves all over him, and Raven was nowhere to be seen "Fine!" he shouted, "I didn't want a dumb cat anyway!" He looked at his hand where Raven bit him, he wasn't sure if he was seeing things or not, but he could have sworn his hand was glowing! "I must have smacked my head hard," he said shaking his hand and head. "I need to get home." He got up and looked around, not knowing which way home was. "Uh-oh," he said, looking frantically around hoping to see something. He started to panic then just started walking in a direction tripping and slipping over sticks and leaves. Ollie started feeling weird as if something around him was happening to him or around him. He rubbed his eyes opening them, he saw everything completely different. Trees look huge, so wide he could barely hug the trunks. The height

on them was so high he felt like he could climb for miles! The flowers looked so colorful he thought he was in a painting, the water rushing by him in the stream sounded like a mighty waterfall when he walked by it.

"Hey, look at the fresh meat," a whisper came from the trees.

"It looks pretty juicy for once, we don't get the big ones very often," another voice whispered.

"Who's there?" Ollie shouted, scared, looking all around him.

"How many do you think it will take to get him?"

"Oh, we will get the whole gang in this. I don't want to lose this one! She will surely love us for bringing her such a feast."

Ollie started backing up. "Who is out there? I don't want any trouble!"

"Oh, don't worry," the voice said, "this won't be any trouble at all, just be very still, and you won't feel a thing."

Ollie squinted hard, up above, he saw a blur in his eyes making all the colors dance all around him, he finally saw something slowly coming down the tree, he froze, crawling down the tree was a spider that was the same size as him! A large slimy grey spider; legs hairy and longer than Ollie's legs, eight black and yellow eyes all looking right at him. Fangs dripping drool as they jump to the ground in front of Ollie. Ollie's skin crawled as he heard all of them creeping around him. He wasn't sure how many were there for he heard them surrounding him, he turned and set his hand on a tree and sunk his hand fully in gooey web. "Oh gross," he shouted pulling with all his might pulling himself free. Laughter echoed the forest as the spiders descended on him for a prize dinner. He screamed, "Get back!" He ran over grabbing a stick and hit one in the leg. "Come on! I'll take you all on!" he shouted swinging his stick. The spider jumped back, but one of the others shot its web and hit the stick out of his hands covered in a gooey web. Ollie rolled away hoping to escape the flurry of web all over. Then *wham*, a large hairy leg hit him in the stomach, sending him flying back right onto a large web covering two big trees. He started squirming and shaking, his heart racing as he's fully stuck inside the web like he's a small fly.

"Now dinner, let us not get too excited!" it said as it walked over drooling.

"Ahhhh, help!" Ollie shouted. Wriggling with all his might unable to get free as a spider dangles from the top drooling all over his head soaking his hair.

The spiders circle him dancing and singing, "*Praise the spider queen. for giving us this dream. It fell into the web, now come you all lets step, oh praise the spider queen!*" They all chant seconds away from enjoying an Ollie lunch, then suddenly, they all hear this deafening roar! Ollie and the spiders look at each other. "Was that you, dinner?" the spider asked.

"No, was that you?" Ollie asked, just as confused.

"Hmm, whatever, where were we," said one of the spiders opening his mouth walking toward Ollie. Suddenly, Ollie saw a huge black blur falling from the tree! Stepping right on the spider about to eat him, squishing it into the ground sending green goo everywhere.

CHAPTER 10

"Let the human. Go he's mine!"

"Raven?" Ollie asked in amazement.

"Get your own lunch, you beast! Let. Him. Go," she said, snarling and stepping closer. One of the spiders ran at her trying to bite her, but she was twice its size, and with one swipe, she swatted the spider far slamming into a tree where it knocked its head.

"Ouch!" it howls. "Get the beast!" As they all started running, Raven hopped over and cut Ollie free with her claws, cutting the web easily as he fell to the ground, whipping a group of spiders with her tail sending them flying. The other spiders climbed the trees regrouping for another attack.

"I don't believe this," Ollie said to Raven as he slowly got up looking into her giant yellow eyes, the small cat now bigger than him, her teeth like daggers, and her paws bigger than his hands.

He petted her side, not believing she was there. "This can't be happening am I dreaming?"

"This is no dream, small human, I saw you fall, and I am sorry I hurt you, but I did that to let you see life the way I see it. This is why everything feels so different, I gave you some of my power. No other living creature has responded the way you have. I will need your help if we are going to clear this forest of evil, for there are too many for me to attack alone."

"This is so amazing!" Ollie shouted. "You were amazing back there scaring them all off."

Raven's ears went back as she turned around. "Do not celebrate just yet, the spiders are coming back with more friends!"

"I need a stick we will show them!'" He rushed over and grabbed a stick off the tree.

"Let me see it," Raven said, walked over, and breathed on it. Suddenly, the stick turned into a sword!

"Whoa," he said, swinging it back and forth. Raven grabbed an acorn and breathed on it making it grow and popping it open, she made Ollie a helmet.

"They are coming back!" he said pointing with his sword.

"Are you ready?" Raven said as she flicked her tail back and forth.

"Let's get them!" Ollie charged, attacking the spiders punching and swinging his sword as Raven pounced all around biting and scratching them, she picked one up and shook it like a toy while Ollie poked one with his sword. Slashing all back and forth, jumping, and twirling in the air.

"This is amazing!" he shouted in glee as he and Raven danced about taking out spider after spider.

"They just keep coming!" Raven said, swatting four spiders away with her paw, watching them tumble away as eight more take their place. Ollie kicked one and ran over by Raven. Looking around, he saw a group of spiders not moving from their spot.

"Look over there!" he said, pointing his sword. "It looks like they are protecting something."

"It has to be the spider queen," Raven said. "They won't stop attacking until they bring us in webs for their queen." Another flurry of spiders rushed the pair. Fighting together, Ollie hit one in the head as Raven batted it away. A spider inches away from biting Raven, Ollie diving over her, tackling it to the ground, grabbing it by the leg and swinging it in circles sending it flying.

"Run!" Raven said as they both take off for a hiding spot. Ollie running with all his might barely catching his breath as they hide behind a tree both panting heavy. Crouching low as he peeks around the spiders looking all around for them, yelling at each other looking for the dinner.

"This is never going to end, how will we ever win?"

"They aren't scared of me enough!" she hissed angrily. "I'm sorry I got you into this, small human, I want you to run away to the house. I will fight them off as long as possible, my battle will be legendary," she said, puffing up, holding up a paw.

"Stop, I'm not going anywhere, we are in this together," Ollie said, petting her head.

"Why would you stay for me? I don't understand this small human. I got you lost, and you don't even want me here you said."

"I know what I said and I'm sorry, I was being a baby. I think I need you as much as you need me right now. You are an alien trapped on this planet, well, the entire time I've been in Colorado, I've felt the same way. I'm an alien to this place. I think we should stick together for survival!"

Raven looked down on him and smiled purring loud. "I'd like that, small human, though it might be a short time if we don't think of a way out of this."

"If only my friends were here! We have been training for something like this" Ollie said, scratching his head. "I've got it!" Ollie said, jumping up thinking about his last mission with his friends. "Follow me, we need to get a closer look."

CHAPTER 11

They started creeping closer in, avoiding any spider they see. He looked up and over the forest and saw the queen sitting on a fallen tree high in the sky covered in the web. "Yes, that looks similar to the tree house," he thought smiling. "Okay, this is what we need to do." He walked over and whispered into her ear the whole plan.

Her eyes got big as she smiled. "This is insane… I love it!"

"Okay, I'll give you a few minutes to get in position, I will hoot at you when it's clear." Raven took off into the trees in the direction of the queen spider. Ollie grabbed his sword and took a deep breath. "I can do this," he whispered. "I am Knight Ollie the Great!" he shouted, holding up his sword, then slamming it down making a loud *crack*! "Hey, over here, you slobber brains!" he said, shouting at all the spiders. "You sure are bad at catching dinner! How have you not starved?"

"Get that little worm!" one of the spiders shouted.

Ollie took off running again and turned his head. "Hey, if you catch me, don't give me to the queen, she looks a little too round, she could lose some weight!"

"He insults the queen!" the spiders all exclaimed. All thirty spiders immediately started chasing after him shouting at him.

Whoa, that worked a little too well, he thought, seeing that many spiders after him, he ran even harder, heart racing, feeling more alive than he ever has. He ran through the trees and turned a sharp corner and stopped in a large clearing, cupping his hands together. "*Coo, coo, coo!*" he yelled at the top of his lungs. About to take off again, all the spiders dropped out of the trees surrounding him.

"You dare talk about our beautiful queen?" A spider spitted out so angry, he's drooling while he talked. "Now you can't escape, you large fly! The queen will enjoy you so much tonight while we dance in glory."

"I don't plan on going down easily," Ollie shouted as he drew his sword grabbing a large piece of bark as a shield. He charged a group of spiders, swinging his shield, hitting one in the head as he slashed another, rolling over, hitting two more. Diving over a log as a spider jumped to bite him, missing him by inches, watching the teeth chatter almost in slow motion as he fell to the ground. Taking off, running in the direction of the queen, he was slamming spiders with his shield, slashing them as he ran. Looking back and smiling, he shouted, "I can do this all day!" Turning back, he ran right into a hairy leg in his way. *Whack!* The spider hit him right on the helmet hard, making him roll dropping his shield and sword. Covered in mud and webs, the spider jumped on him pinning him down.

"Yes, I have caught you! The queen will love me most!" The other spiders ran over surrounding him.

"Get away!" Ollie tried to punch them, but the spider started shooting web all over his arms and legs covering him, making him unable to move.

"The dinner is caught!" all the spiders shouted, laughing and dancing all around Ollie, singing their song over and over as they picked him up, carrying him to the queen.

CHAPTER 12

They carried him to the base of the queen's tree, laughing, dancing, and singing on how brave and awesome they were catching such a big fly. "My queen, I have brought you the feast of a lifetime!" the spider said, dropping Ollie down on the ground. They could not see or hear her, all of them went quiet.

"My queen? Come down and feast on this delicious meal" They heard a loud *crack* and a roar.

"No thanks, I just found a lovely meal up here!" a voice shouted.

"Who's up there?" the spider said nervously. Raven jumped down with the queen in her mouth.

"The Queen!" they all gasped as Raven chomped down eating her in one bite.

"A little crunchy but not too bad!" Raven said, burping out the queen's crown in front of the spiders. "Now who's going to be dessert?" as she roars as loud as she can. All the spiders screamed, shaking, all running back deeper into the forest.

"Who was that beast? She ate the queen."

Raven jumped to a high log. "I am Raven, Dark Lord of All! Fear me!" she roared again, sending the rest of the spiders far away until the forest was silent.

"We did it!" Ollie said, still bound up in web.

Raven walked over to Ollie and cut him free. "You did great back there, small human," Raven said, licking her giant paw.

"I never would have thought of making a diversion to attack the queen, how did you know it would work?"

"Well, let's just say you aren't the only being here with brains and power," Ollie said laughing. "How are you so big? he asked looking at her.

"As I told you before, I'm a being of magical greatness. I can do whatever I want! But to not scare you, I will retain my normal cat size." Raven began to shrink down in size as they started walking back home.

"I cannot wait to tell Mom and Dad what just happened. This was the coolest day ever!"

"No, small human, remember, you can't tell your parents what happened, my mission is top secret, they cannot know of anything that happened here today. They will not understand and will not want you in the danger of my missions. We alien need to stick together right?" she said, smiling at Ollie.

"Okay, I guess you are right. We can keep it a secret for now," Ollie said, rolling his eyes.

"Thank you, small human," she said back as a small cat trotting by Ollie.

"You know you can call me Ollie, right?"

"You are right. My apologies, Small Ollie."

"What, no, just Ollie, no small," he said, looking at her sternly.

"Small Ollie is fine I don't mind," Raven said, chuckling as she walked by him.

CHAPTER 13

"Ollie, supper will be ready soon," Mom said, walking into his room and gasping. "Ollie, look at you! You are filthy! I just bought those clothes for you! Get in the tub this minute, young man!" Mom shouted, pulling sticks and leaves out of his hair, looking at the trail of dirt all over the house. "Oh, my soul, Ollie, what on earth did you get into out there?"

"I was saving the forest from a spider invasion, Mom!" Ollie said, running to the bathroom, stripping off his dirty clothes.

Ollie was sitting in the tub full of bubbles, washing his hair; Raven was sitting on the edge of the tub. "So why are you here, Raven?" Ollie said, rubbing bubbles on this chin to make a beard.

"I am here because my spaceship crashed as I was on my way home. I don't know what happened, I remember my crew and I were just back from a recon mission when a giant red light blinded us all, next thing I remember is waking up in a small cage a few days before your big human brought me here."

"Whoa," Ollie said in awe.

"I need to find my ship soon. I need to get a message to the high leaders of my people, what we found is world changing!"

"What is it?" Ollie asked, drying off looking at Raven.

"I can't tell you now, but once we find my ship, I will bring you with me, and we will complete my mission."

"Awesome, I want to fly the ship!" Ollie said, drying off and putting on fresh clothes.

Raven laughed. "As if I would let you fly a level five-star glob transporter on your first take off," still chuckling as she walked up the stairs.

"Ollie, supper time!" Mom said, setting the table as Dad walked in the door.

CHAPTER 14

Mom, Dad, and Ollie all sitting at the table looked over at Raven as she walked over and sat in the empty chair beside Ollie and patted a piece of shrimp on his plate. "Give me, please," she whispered. All of them laughing as he gave her a piece.

"So, bud, how was your day? Mom said you and Princess went outside, or I mean Raven now is it?"

Ollie lit up. "Oh, Dad, it was so awesome. The backyard is big, we found the spiders you were talking about, they were huge! We kicked their butts, so you don't need to worry about anything. Raven, and I will keep it safe back there, the queen is of no more concern, let's just say that," Ollie said, winking at the little black cat.

"The queen?" Dad asked, confused. Raven set a paw on Ollie's leg and pushed her claws out.

"Ow!" he said, looking at her as she squinted at him. "Oh, nothing, Dad, just know we took care of the big spiders in the back.

"Well, thanks, buddy, that marks something of my list of chores." Dad laughed, patting Ollie's back. "I'm glad you and her finally started playing together and are keeping us safe. Cats aren't so bad now, are they?"

"They are pretty cool, Dad, I never thanked you for getting me a friend for the summer. I know I was mean to you and Mom about moving to Colorado. I am sorry for how I acted. I will miss my friends, but I think I am starting to like Colorado. Me and Raven will have plenty of fun this summer!" Mom and Dad looked at each other smiling, sighing in relief.

"That's great, sweetie, we are really glad you are liking it here now," Mom said as she walked over, getting dessert. "I forgot to tell you, but you cousin Jensa is coming here in a week to spend a month with us. I told your aunt you were sad here, and we thought it might be fun having her here with you."

"That's amazing, I can't wait! Thank you so much!" Ollie ran over and hugged his mom.

As they were cleaning the kitchen when the doorbell rang, Mom walked over and opened the door. "Ollie it's for you," Mom said.

Ollie ran up the stairs confused and saw Steve and Victoria at the door.

"Hey," he said shyly, remembering the embarrassment that happened earlier.

"Hey, Ollie, so Victoria told me what actually happened today, I'm sorry I yelled at you and told you to leave. Today was incredibly stressful trying to get Tucker settled. That's what I named my dog," Steve said.

"Whoa, that's the name I was going to name my dog too! And it's okay, I hope I didn't bother you too much."

"You didn't bother us at all, Ollie," Victoria said smiling. "I hope we can hang out more now that we are neighbors. Don't worry, Jonathan won't be around much now, he has to go to summer school," she said, covering her mouth, giggling.

"Well, if your parents are okay with it, you are more than welcome to come over in a few weeks once Tucker is settled in, he's actually a really sweet dog and is great around kids," Steve said, looking at Ollie's mom.

"Oh, absolutely, I see no problem with that, you both are adorable," Mom said smiling.

"Great, well, we will see you later, Ollie," Steve said, turning to walk away.

"Yeah, see you later, Ollie." Victoria stepped in, giving him a hug. "We are excited to have you here in Colorado, you will love it here!" Then she took off running. Ollie closed the door, Mom was behind him smiling.

"Aww, so who was that?" she said winking at Ollie.

Ollie turned red. "Go away, Mom, you are weird," he said, laughing running back to his room.

That night in bed, Ollie was looking at the ceiling, sat up, and looked at Raven. "Why did you save me?" The cat snorted awake, wiping drool from her whiskers.

"What?" she said dazedly.

"Why did you save me? I would have been spider food if it weren't for you."

She stood up and stretched walking over to him curling up by his neck. "Because even though you are a small human, I still think you are worth having as part of my crew. Today, I looked all over the forest, and I found nothing but danger and enemies, I will need your help if I am to complete my mission. Are you ready to go on some adventures and help me save my world?" Raven said lazily as she dozed off.

"You bet I am," Ollie whispered as they both fell asleep, resting up for what tomorrow will bring them.

CHAPTER 15

Raven opened her eye looking to see if Ollie was asleep. She slowly crept out of the bed and went to the window and opened it. Hovering outside was a small craft the shape of an egg glowing. "Raven, Dark Lord of All," she said to the egg.

"Voice identification accepted," the egg chirped in a robotic voice. It opened into a large screen. Mission report it typed out. She went over typing on the keyboard of her language:

Ravens log, Star date 2020 Glorp date 5455991

I have successfully disguised myself as a small creature to integrate with these life-forms called humans. In efforts to keep our people safe, I recommend we all use this guise whenever dealing with the earthlings. I was skeptical of my mission heading here to observe, but these seem to be a very interesting case study; they are big and squishy and are easily distracted by small light boxes and use water to clean their bodies instead of their tongues. Definitely not as advanced as our own race, but I will continue my work and will report my findings to see if they are the right species to help us in our most trying time. I feel confident in this Ollie, his bravery and smarts today surprised me in the way he handled his first mission with me. Obviously, I knew how to handle the entire mission myself easily, but he may just be the advantage we need in the ongoing war. Will update mission control when I have more intel. Raven, out.

The screen beeped, "Message received, be warned, Bounty Hunter Karen will be arriving to assist soon. Will update you when she is on the way via teleportation, mission control out." The screen closed, and the egg shot into the night sky far into space. Raven flattened her ears and let out a sigh. "Not Karen the bounty hunter, we were such rivals at the academy. This mission just got a lot harder with that hot head on her way," Raven muttered as she closed the window and jumped back on the bed and curled up on Ollie's neck again. "You are my last hope, Ollie, do not let me down," Raven said, worried as she drifted to sleep.

ABOUT THE AUTHOR

D. C. Whitlock was born in Charleston, South Carolina, but moved quite a bit for the first ten years of his life until he and his family settled in Colorado. He grew up having pets his whole life, mainly cats and dogs. Today, D. C. resides in Colorado Springs with his two cats, Raven and Karen.

CPSIA information can be obtained
at www.ICGtesting.com
Printed in the USA
BVHW050943221121
622229BV00015B/476